Disney's Aladdin
The Cave of Wonders

Adapted by Ann Braybrooks
Illustrated by Phil Ortiz and Darrell Baker

A Golden Book • New York
Western Publishing Company, Inc., Racine, Wisconsin 53404

 Library of Congress Catalog Card Number: 92-73720 ISBN: 0-307-11565-8/ISBN: 0-307-65655-1 (lib. bdg.)   A MCMXCIII

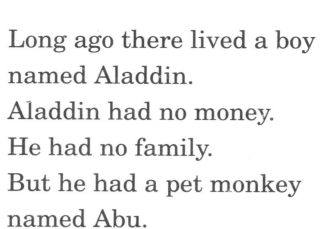

Long ago there lived a boy
named Aladdin.
Aladdin had no money.
He had no family.
But he had a pet monkey
named Abu.

One day Aladdin and Abu
met an old man.
The old man promised them
a great treasure.
But first Aladdin had to go into a cave
and bring out a magic lamp.

Aladdin stepped into the cave.
A deep voice boomed,
"You may enter.
But you must not touch the treasure.
Touch only the lamp!"

Aladdin and Abu went down the stairs.

The cave was filled with treasure.

"Wow!" said Aladdin.

"Look at all this stuff!"

Abu's eyes got big.

He wanted some treasure.

And he wanted it now!

Abu ran to a treasure chest.

"Do not touch!" Aladdin cried.
"We have to find the lamp!"
Abu pulled his hand back.

Abu and Aladdin went
deeper into the cave.
They were all alone.
Or were they?
Tap, tap!
Something tapped Abu
on the shoulder.

Abu turned around
and saw a carpet.
A magic carpet!
Abu was scared.
"Aiii!" he cried.
Now the carpet was scared.
It flew away and hid.

"Come back, carpet,"
Aladdin called.
"We will not hurt you."
The carpet slowly crept out.

"Can you help us find
the magic lamp?"
Aladdin asked.
The carpet nodded
and showed them the way.

Soon they came to another cavern.
"There is the lamp!" cried Aladdin.
"Stay here, Abu.
Do not touch anything!"

13

Aladdin crossed the water.
He climbed to the top
of a high staircase.
The magic lamp was
finally in reach.

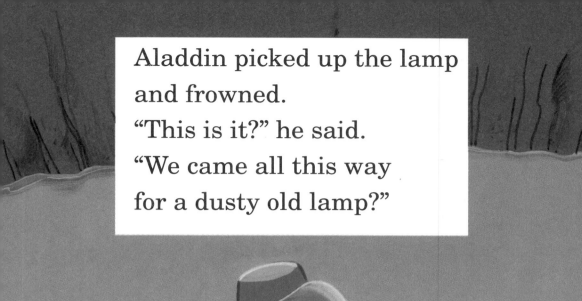

Aladdin picked up the lamp
and frowned.
"This is it?" he said.
"We came all this way
for a dusty old lamp?"

Abu was not looking at the lamp.
He was looking at a big ruby.
It sparkled.
It gleamed.

Abu reached for the ruby.
The carpet tried to hold him back.

Just then Aladdin turned
around and saw Abu.
"No, Abu!" he cried.
"Do not touch that ruby!"
But it was too late.
Abu had grabbed the jewel.

The ground shook.
The walls rumbled.
The water
turned to lava.
Aladdin held the lamp
as he fell toward the boiling sea.

Whoosh!
Just in time the carpet swooped
under Aladdin.
Then it caught Abu, too.

The cave was shaking apart.
The carpet carried them
as far as the cave entrance.
The stairs were disappearing!

Aladdin and Abu
tried to climb.
The old man was
waiting at the top.

"Help me out!"
Aladdin called to the old man.
"Give me the lamp first!"
the old man cried.

Aladdin handed over the lamp.
But the old man did not help him!
He made Aladdin fall back into the cave.

Abu was very angry.

He attacked the old man.

The old man grabbed Abu

and tossed him back into the cave.

The old man smiled an evil smile.

Down, down, down
fell Aladdin and Abu.
The carpet tried
to catch them again.
But this time all three
hit the cave floor.

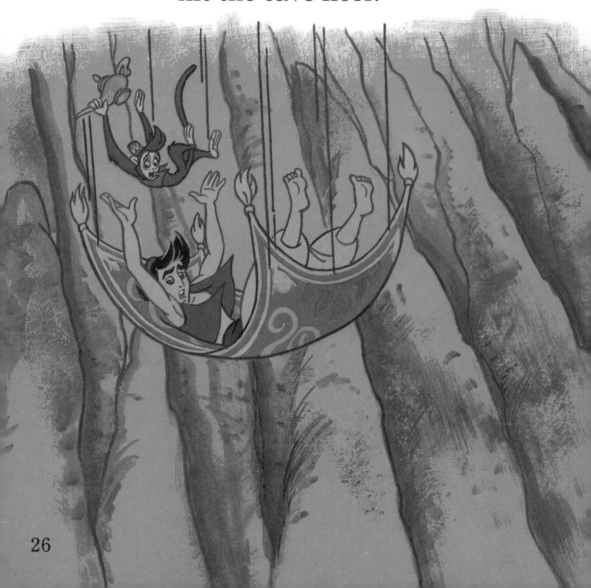

"Ouch!" said Aladdin.
He rubbed his head.
Then Abu jumped up
and showed him the lamp.
Abu had grabbed it away
from the old man!

Aladdin looked up.
The cave entrance was blocked.
Then he looked around
the cold, dark cave.
"We are trapped," he said.
"All because of a lamp!"
He rubbed the dusty lamp . . .

and a genie appeared!

"Hello, master!" said the Genie.
Aladdin did not know what to say.
But he thought fast.

"Most genies have magic powers,"
Aladdin said.

"Can *you* get us out of this cave?"

"You bet!" the Genie said.

The Genie used his magic
to make an opening in the cave.
Then they all flew out
on the magic carpet.
"I am glad I found the lamp!"
said Aladdin.
"Now I have a genie of my own!"